Dash is a New Fooder!

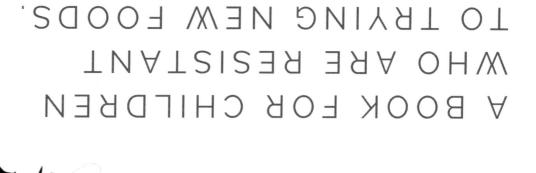

New Fooder!

A BOOK FOR CHILDREN WHO ARE RESISTANT TO TRYING NEW FOODS.

Dash is a New Fooder!, written and illustrated by Wendy Hayden
SWH Medial LLC.
www.NaturalConstipationSolutions.com
© 2019 Wendy Hayden
Cover by Wendy Hayden

Dash Learns
Life Skills
Series

"Dash, you're spending the day with Grandma.
Pick up your toys." said Mama.

"Yay! I love to visit Grandma!" said Dash.

Dash was so excited to see Grandma that
he didn't mind picking up his toys.

Dash ran to Grandma and gave her a big kiss.

"I'm so happy to see you, Grandma!"

Grandma said, "Dash, I'm so happy to see you, too!"

After Mama left to go to the store,
Grandma read a book to Dash.

Grandma asked "Dash, would you like a snack?"

"Yes, Grandma.'" said Dash. "I would love a snack!"

Grandma asked "What would you like?"

"A candy bar?"
answered Dash.

Grandma said, "Oh Dash! I wasn't
thinking about that kind of snack."

"I have apples, pears or celery. Which would you like, Dash?"

"But those are all green, Grandma!" said Dash.

"Green foods are good for you, Dash. It is important to eat things that will make you healthy and strong. What if I put peanut butter on the celery?" asked Grandma."

"I like peanut butter but I don't want celery."said Dash.

"Don't be a No New Fooder, Dash." said Grandma.

"Ok, Grandma, I guess I'll try it." said Dash.

Dash licked the peanut butter but he didn't eat the celery.

"Now Dash, don't be a No New Fooder!" said Grandma.

Dash took a bite of the celery.

It was crunchy and tasted pretty good!

Celery with peanut butter
is a yummy snack!

Grandma and Dash went outside to play. Dash had so much fun playing ball with Grandma.

Dash played hard. He was tired and really hungry.

Dash was happy when Grandma said it was time for lunch.

Dash couldn't wait for lunch.

Dash wondered what Grandma was going to feed him.

Grandma brought in plates filled with all new foods.

Dash wasn't sure about this.....

Grandma asked "What's wrong, Dash?"

"I don't want this lunch, Grandma." said Dash.

"I want Chicken Nuggets or Macaroni & Cheese or Pizza!"

"Dash, I know those foods taste good. They are ok to have sometimes. But your body needs you to eat foods with lots of different colors to make your body strong and healthy."

"Grandma, I eat lots of colors!
My favorite cereal has lots of colors."

"Dash, those aren't the types of colors that I mean."

"You need the colors to come from fruits and vegetables, not from food coloring."

"Red, purple, green, yellow and orange foods have vitamins and minerals that keep you healthy and strong." said Grandma.

"Well, Pizza is red and macaroni and cheese is...orange and.... "
But everything else Dash liked to eat was either tan or white.
He couldn't think of any other colorful food he liked.

Grandma said "Try one bite of each thing on your plate and see what you think. You don't want to be a No New Fooder!"

Broccoli tasted yummy.

And it was fun to eat!

Dash felt like a dinosaur eating a tree!

Dash decided that he really liked

colorful

new food!

When Dash's Mama came to pick him up,
Grandma told her all of the new colorful foods he had tried.
Mama and Grandma were proud of their New Fooder!

Dash was proud to be a
New Fooder, too!

Visit

NaturalConstipationSolutions.com/NewFooder

for free activities to help your
No New Fooder become a proud New Fooder.

Also available:
Dash's Belly Ache
A book for children
who can't
or won't poop

Made in the USA
Monee, IL
11 August 2020